Romeo and Juliet

ABOUT THE AUTHOR

Beverley Birch grew up in Kenya and first came to England, where she now lives with her husband and two daughters, at the age of fifteen. After completing an MA in Economics and Sociology, Beverley became an editor at Penguin. Within a few weeks she was offered the chance to work on children's books and has been involved in children's publishing – as both editor and writer – ever since.

She has had over forty books published, from picture books and novels to science biographies and retellings of classic works. All her titles have received critical acclaim and her work has been translated into more than a dozen languages. Her latest novel for teenagers, *Rift*, was published in 2006.

Shakespeare's Tales

Romeo
and Juliet

Retold by Beverley Birch

Illustrated by Jenny Williams

WAYLAND

For my mother, with love

Text copyright © 1988 Beverley Birch
Illustrations copyright © 2006 Jenny Williams

First published in *Shakespeare's Stories: Tragedies* in 1988 by
Macdonald & Co (Publishers) Limited.
This edition first published in 2006 by
Wayland, an imprint of Hachette Children's Books

Cover and text design: Rosamund Saunders

Hachette Children's Books
338 Euston Road, London NW1 3BH

Printed and bound in the United Kingdom

ISBN-10: 0 7502 4966 8
ISBN-13: 978 0 7502 4966 9

The Cast

THE HOUSE OF MONTAGUE
Old Montague
Lady Montague
Romeo – their son
Benvolio – Romeo's friend
Friar Lawrence – friend and adviser to Romeo

THE HOUSE OF CAPULET
Old Capulet
Lady Capulet
Juliet – their daughter
Nurse – friend and adviser to Juliet
Tybalt – Juliet's cousin

The Prince of Verona
Paris – a relative of the prince
Mercutio – a relative of the prince and
friend of Romeo

Within the ancient walls of fair Verona lived two families, the Capulets and the Montagues. Both, alike, were rich and honoured in the city, but both alike were poisoned by a hatred that festered deep within them. Its cause was lost long in the distant past. Only the vicious anger lingered, like the rotten odour of a crime, polluting both the families.

Capulets hated Montagues, and Montagues hated Capulets: each son and daughter, cousin, uncle, aunt, each servant, cat and dog had bred the venom deep into their veins. Twice already in the blistering heat of this high summer their quarrel boiled to vicious brawls across the narrow streets and sleepy squares. Now it flared again: two bored servants of the house of Capulet taunted two servants of the Montagues, and in a flash the swords and daggers sliced amid the snarlings of wild men, like savage animals.

A young Montague named Benvolio rushed to part the struggling men; Tybalt, a young Capulet who burned for every chance to vent his fury on a Montague, leapt out into the fray. Within minutes the street was filled with Montague fighting Capulet, while women of the city hurried children in behind closed doors and pulled the shutters down against the chopping swords. And once again

Verona's citizens drew rusty weapons
from retirement and ran out to part the
foes who seemed to have no other aim in
life except to butcher one another.

There was one of the house of
Montague who did not flourish a sword
that day. Young Romeo was far from that
blighted scene, plunged in a moody
solitude. Benvolio, still panting from his
efforts as a peace-maker at the brawl,
met brooding Romeo wandering across
the square and joined him, anxious
to discover why his cousin shunned
all company.

It was not difficult to tap the cause of
Romeo's ache: he longed to tell. He
pined for love! A lady, Rosaline by name,

bewitched him with her beauty, but would not return his love …

Benvolio was quick with good advice. 'Be ruled by me,' he urged his cousin Romeo. 'Forget to think of her! Examine other beauties.'

Romeo would have none of this. He wanted to remain locked in his love-sick melancholy. Forget Rosaline? He could never forget the precious treasure of her beauty!

Old Capulet was in an affable mood. Verona's prince had dealt fairly enough with him after the brawl that afternoon. Both he and Montague were bound now, on pain of death, to keep the city's peace. And it seemed to Capulet that it should not be hard for men as old as they to try, at least. More important questions filled his mind today. A young nobleman named Paris had asked for his daughter's hand in marriage! Though his daughter, Juliet, was very young to be a bride, for she had not yet turned fourteen, there could not possibly be a better suitor than this noble man. Wealthy, handsome, well-connected (he was a relative of the prince), he was the perfect husband for a daughter.

So Capulet had given permission to young Paris to woo Juliet that very night; for Capulet was giving a ball, an annual, traditional feast to which all his friends and relatives would come.

'Go, sirrah,' he told his new servant, beaming with benevolent good-humour, 'trudge about through fair Verona; find out those persons whose names are written on this list, and say to them my house and welcome await their pleasure!'

But the servant could not read. And so it was that Romeo and Benvolio, still strolling the dusty streets together, were shown this Capulet invitation list and asked to read the names on it, the servant little guessing that he asked the favour of two Montagues.

Seeing the list of names, Benvolio saw at once a merry plot to shake cousin Romeo from his gloom. The fair Rosaline

would be at the Capulet feast. So would
other admired beauties of Verona. If
Romeo could be persuaded to go there,
he could compare the haughty Rosaline
with others! He clapped his arm about
his cousin's shoulders. 'I will make you
think your swan a crow!' he assured
him confidently.

Half-enticed by this daring proposition,
Romeo agreed to go. But only, he
warned, so he could feast his eyes on
Rosaline's splendour …

In the Capulet household there was
much fluttering of silks and ribbons,
much preening, brushing, smoothing,
polishing, much rushing up and down for

plates piled high with delicacies, and much cursing of the Nurse who kept disappearing with the pantry keys.

Juliet soared with anticipation of the feast's delights. What more excitement could there be than her own home alive with friends, ringing with merriment, a-gleam with party finery?

Her mother told her that young Paris sought her hand in marriage (a fine gentleman, so handsome, held in high esteem, a most worthy husband – her mother and her Nurse waxed lyrical on Paris' virtues) and Juliet agreed to look at him, at least.

But marriage was not in Juliet's thoughts. She felt too young, too much in love with music, dance and song, to think of marriage.

Behind their comic masks and gorgeous, gaudy costumes, the young Montagues came boldly to the Capulet feast, for it was the custom of the day that uninvited guests, disguised, could swell the numbers of a ball and so enhance the joyful mystery of the occasion.

They came through streets that flickered with the firefly flames of torches and danced with the shadows of other maskers flitting to the ball. Yet Romeo was out of sorts with this light-hearted quest for merriment, and Mercutio,

his dear and closest friend, worked hard
to tease him from his persistent mood
of gloom.

'Gentle Romeo. We must have you
dance!' he chided him. 'You are a lover;
borrow Cupid's wings and soar with
them …'

Romeo would not be stung to lightness
by such mockery, insisting that he be only
a torchbearer at the ball and look on,
perhaps to catch a glimpse of Rosaline.

But bubbling Mercutio, whose darting
wit would never quake before the
mysteries of life, only teased at them now,
just as he teased Romeo.

'I see Queen Mab has been with you!' he
winked and nodded knowingly. 'She is the

fairies' midwife,' solemnly he explained, 'and she comes in shape no bigger than a precious jewel on the forefinger of a councillor, drawn by a team of tiny creatures across men's noses as they lie asleep. Her chariot is an empty hazelnut made by the squirrel and in this state she gallops, night by night, through lovers' brains, and then they dream of love!'

'Peace, peace, Mercutio, peace!' begged Romeo, half-laughing with him now. 'You talk of nothing …'

'True, I talk of dreams …' nodded Mercutio.

But Romeo had been having dreams of a different sort. His wistful dream of Rosaline had been pierced the night

before by something more than the
hopeless yearnings of unanswered love.
Something more fearful beckoned him,
beyond his reach, as though it warned of
some grim process which would begin its
march with this night's revels and would
lead by a cold, haunting path, to death …

In the great ballroom of his house old
Capulet stood smiling a genial
welcome to his guests, urging them to
drink and feast and the musicians to
strike up a merry note for all to dance.
He offered a cordial hand to the
company of maskers who came to grace
his ball, and Mercutio and Benvolio were
swept away on the wings of gaiety. Amid

the twinkling lights and gleaming floors, soft-slippered feet pranced and danced to the swish of silks and velvets. But Romeo saw nothing of this scene. He had seen a vision he had never seen before, a girl of such exquisite beauty …

He had seen Juliet. Across the dancing room her glow had caught him in its light and put all thought of Rosaline to instant flight. Juliet seemed to burn with such radiance that all else receded into glowing dark: Romeo saw nothing but her gleaming hair and shining eyes …

In rapt wonder he stood watching her. Dare he move closer?

Tybalt saw the young masker watch his cousin Juliet as though his eyes would never drink enough, and he became suspicious. He drew near, heard Romeo's voice enquiring of a passing servant who the stranger was, and anger shot through him with age-old viciousness.

'This by his voice should be a Montague,' he breathed. 'Fetch me a sword!' he told a servant. How dare a Montague invade a Capulet house, disguised, and sneer at their revelling!

Old Capulet saw his fiery nephew arming for some fight and hurried forward. Not at this feast! Not in this house!

'I'll not endure him,' hissed Tybalt, throwing off his uncle's hand.

'He shall be endured! *I* say he shall!' thundered Capulet. 'Am I master here, or

you? You'll make a mutiny among my
guests! You are an insolent youth. Be
quiet, or I'll make you quiet.'

Flaming with thwarted hate, Tybalt
withdrew. But he had not given up. He
would still find his time to challenge this
Montague who thumbed his nose at them!

Blind to the struggle being waged so
near at hand, Romeo had drawn close to
Juliet. Across the bobbing heads of
dancers Juliet had seen the mysterious
young man who seemed to glide towards
her as if some witchcraft beyond his power
propelled him on. The wonderment that
shone even from his hidden face, touched
an answering, slumbering flame in her.
She looked, and she was captured.

She waited for him, enthralled. Their hands touched, shyly. There were half-humorous words exchanged which glowed with hidden meaning for the two, who had no eyes for anyone else in that enchanted room, no ears for any music now, but that which played within their own ears and eyes and hearts.

Romeo begged a kiss. Shyly, Juliet gave it. And then again, as though there was no time but this sweet moment, no place but that in which they stood together.

And then the world broke through and she was swept away in the broad encircling arms of Nurse to see her mother.

Who was she, this guest in Capulet's house? Romeo longed to know. But she

was no guest, she was the only daughter
of old Capulet.

Romeo's heart missed a beat. The only
daughter of his father's enemy! Was he to
stare at her across the chasm of hatred
which split Montague from Capulet by a
century of spilling blood?

Old Capulet, watching the masked
Montagues prepare to leave, was far
from fuelling this ancient war. He felt
too filled with merry humour, for tonight
young Paris had come to woo his
daughter, Juliet!

Stay, he urged the Montagues, giving
no sign that he knew who they were. But
they set off, and Juliet, lingering to watch,
sent Nurse to ask the stranger's name;

and so she learned that it was Romeo, a Montague, the only son of her own family's greatest enemy.

'My only love sprung from my only hate!' she gasped, for a moment appalled by it. But she would not let this evening's magic be dimmed! She gave no eyes to anything but the masked stranger, who departed with a backward look of longing that answered her own.

Benvolio and Mercutio had left the party and seen Romeo go on ahead of them. Now they could find him nowhere. They called. They teased. 'Romeo! Madman! Passion! Lover!' Mercutio called. He tried to conjure him by all the tricks that he could muster: by Rosaline's bright eyes, by her high forehead and her scarlet lip (for they knew nothing of the swift flight of Romeo's old love and the instant birth of his new). But still Romeo was nowhere to be found, and so, rollicking with good cheer and bawdy humour, the two friends rolled on their way home.

Yet Romeo was near, and heard them. He had gone ahead and on an impulse leapt the wall into old Capulet's orchard. Shocked by this surge of daring, he hid from his friends' mockery. Now, in the darkness, he crouched down, not knowing why he stayed or what he hoped to do, but propelled by that same unseen power of fascination towards the house where dazzling Juliet lived.

It was as if the darkness was suddenly aflame, for Juliet stepped out on to her balcony, and then it seemed to Romeo's eyes as though she was the sun rising to flood the world with glorious light.

An impulse pushed him forward, then he held back. He struggled with the wish to run to her and then to hide in shyness and just drink in the wondrous vision.

Juliet, on her balcony, was unaware of watching eyes. She sighed loudly, for she was wrestling with the misery of knowing that her passionate stranger was a Montague.

'Deny your father,' she begged, as

though Romeo lodged somewhere in the rustling tree-tops. 'Refuse your name! Or if you will not, be my love and I'll no longer be a Capulet. It is your name that is my enemy. Oh, be some other name!' she addressed the moon and stars. 'What's in a name! If we call a rose by any other name it would smell as sweet. So would Romeo were he not called Romeo. Romeo, throw off your name, and take all myself!' she cried, abandoning herself to this secret dialogue with unseen love.

Romeo broke from the shadow of the wall. 'Call me but love,' he cried, 'and I'll be new baptized, I will be Romeo no more!'

With a cry Juliet fled back into the

shadows, aghast at being watched when she believed she was alone. But realizing who the secret visitor was, she stepped forward, timidly, peeped, grew bolder and moved to look down across the balcony wall and see him.

'If my family sees you, they will murder you,' she warned him, softly, but letting her eyes caress his face so warmly that he felt armed against any Capulet dagger.

So they stood there, bathed in the moonlight that silver-tipped the fruit-tree tops, drunk with their new-made vows of love. For Juliet's heart was yet untapped, and though she knew her father brewed a marriage with Paris for her, she was bewitched by this mysterious young man who had, unasked, pierced the seclusion of her life, broken all the boundaries that divided this ancient, hate-locked city, and crossed forbidden territory to her side. *This* was not a love wrapped up in good sense and handed to her by a father, mother, Nurse, or any other. *This* love was hers, and even as they gave their first vows to each other, it entered her soul with a fierce passion that would never leave her.

'My bounty is as boundless as the sea,' she cried. 'My love as deep; the more I give to you, the more I have, for both are infinite!'

Romeo knew he could live in the magic of this night for ever. It seemed as though he had drifted from a wilderness in which he ached always alone, a pilgrim in a thankless search for love: (how long it seemed to be since he had thought he ached for Rosaline!). But now it was as though his whole existence led towards this single night, and nothing could exist outside. All time was now, he and Juliet locked in their bond of faith; there was no future and no past, except with her.

Quickly, before the world intrude with the dawn and take from them anything of their sworn love, he hurried to a monastery outside the city walls to see the monk, Friar Lawrence, who knew him well.

The friar was shocked to find young Romeo already up, and quickly guessed he had not been to bed that night. But learning that this excess of energy was not devoted to the lovely Rosaline, he was amazed to hear another girl had stolen in to take her place. He shook his head. Young men's love did not lie truly in their hearts, but in their eyes! What a tide of tears had Romeo shed for Rosaline, and look now – forgotten!

Romeo would have no scoldings at his fickleness. He had a single-minded purpose now. With all the speed that he could muster, Friar Lawrence must marry him to Juliet, and marry them today!

The friar stared, half disbelieving what he heard. This doting youth was so changeable he could not keep up with him! Yet, watching Romeo prowl up and down in a restless torment of excitement, he hoped that perhaps some deeper flame now spurred his young friend on.

Well, perhaps he should perform this marriage for the youth. Perhaps Capulets and Montagues would even cancel out their hate when such a love could fly the boundary between them!

Benvolio and Mercutio were puzzled. They had not seen Romeo since he left the feast, and he had not gone home that night. Yet they knew that Tybalt, the angry Capulet, had sent a letter to Romeo's house challenging him to a duel for insolence in coming to their ball!

'Romeo will answer it,' said Benvolio, certain of his cousin.

'Alas, poor Romeo!' mourned Mercutio, clasping his heart. 'He is already dead, stabbed with a young girl's black eye, shot through the ear with a love-song … And is he a man to encounter Tybalt?'

'Why, what is Tybalt?' Benvolio enquired.

'More than a prince of cats, I can tell you,' Mercutio waxed lyrical in scorn. 'He is the very butcher of a silk button, a duellist, a gentleman of the very first house, a man of fancy thrusts and lunges,' and he mimicked the self-important prancing steps of Tybalt.

But here came Romeo to interrupt
their joke. And what a change there was!
No longer the mooning youth of
yesterday, but the Romeo of old, so quick
and apt to exchange the cut and thrust of
jest with them that Mercutio retired,
defeated, from the contest, pleased to see
his friend so thoroughly repaired in
spirits. And so they strolled on, chatting,
while Romeo nursed his precious secret
knowledge and looked for some
messenger from Juliet, for she had said
that she would send one.

And here came Nurse, puffing across
the square, fanning away the steaming
heat, and pressing on, for though she
knew that Capulet had already promised

Juliet to Paris, her old heart warmed to this tale of secret love and she thrilled to be Juliet's messenger to Romeo.

Entrusted in the care of Nurse, then, Romeo sent word to Juliet. She must find some way to come to Friar Lawrence's cell that very afternoon. There the holy friar would marry them at once.

Juliet paced up and down as though every minute was an hour and every hour a day until she heard from Romeo. A thousand terrors filled her heart: perhaps Nurse had not yet found him; perhaps she brought bad news; perhaps he'd changed his mind and did not love her …

But when she heard the news all terrors fled, and only the prospect of her union with Romeo lived in her mind. So many hours to go till then!

At Lawrence's cell, Romeo awaited her arrival with scarcely less intensity of hope: there was no sorrow could undo the joy he won from one short minute in Juliet's sight. 'Then love-devouring death do what he dare!' he defied the world. 'It is enough I may call her mine!'

'These violent delights have violent ends,' the friar chided him, 'and in their triumph, they die. Love moderately,' he warned.

But when Juliet came, with an airy step that floated on the cushion of her love, the friar's misgivings were instantly dispelled. Truly these young people loved!

'Come,' he hurried them, 'and we will make short work.' They must be married now, for such a pair should not be held apart.

The heat hung leaden in the streets, damp, cloying, maddening.

Benvolio was nervous, for Mercutio was in a brazen mood, his wit stung to an irritable edge; and there were Capulets drifting through the streets looking for a fight. 'I pray you, good Mercutio, let's go

in,' he begged. 'These hot days the mad blood is stirring.'

'Come, come, you are as hot in your mood as any in Italy,' Mercutio said restlessly, 'and as soon moved to be moody.'

'By my head, here come the Capulets,' Benvolio muttered.

'By my heel, I do not care,' retorted Mercutio, and turned his back on the approaching group.

'Gentlemen,' cried Tybalt, recognizing them as friends of Romeo, 'a word with one of you.'

'But one word with one of us?' said Mercutio, bristling. 'Couple it with something; make it a word and a blow!'

Benvolio tried to pull him back: away, into some private place to have their quarrel, for here all men's eyes were on them, and the prince had forbidden such brawling on pain of the heaviest punishment!

But Tybalt had lost interest in this sparring match, for he saw Romeo enter the square. 'Romeo!' he yelled. 'You are a villain!'

Romeo was fresh from his marriage to Juliet; he knew nothing of the challenge from this cousin of hers and he could find no anger in his heart even to rebuff the open venom of the words. 'I am no villain,' he spoke mildly. 'Therefore, farewell. I see you do not know me.'

'Boy,' spat Tybalt, ripe with insults, 'this shall not excuse the injuries you have done me. Therefore turn and draw your weapon!'

'I do protest,' persisted Romeo, 'I never injured you.' Even now his head was filled with nothing other than his marriage; it made him now a cousin to this Tybalt who pranced so desperately in search of a war. 'So, good Capulet, which name I hold as dearly as my own …'

Mercutio turned on his friend in disbelief. What had become of him, so calmly, so *dishonourably* to submit to this puppet duellist's taunts? Well, he would take the wretched insult up!

'Tybalt, you rat-catcher,' he yelled, and

drew his sword.

And suddenly there they were, circling like wild cats …

'What would you have with me?' snarled Tybalt.

'Good king of cats, nothing but one of your nine lives … ' jeered Mercutio.

'Gentle Mercutio, put your sword away,' urged Romeo.

'Come sir,' Mercutio egged Tybalt on.

'Tybalt, Mercutio, the prince expressly has forbidden fighting in Verona streets,' Romeo cried out. 'Hold Tybalt! Good Mercutio!' and he stepped towards his friend to beat his weapon down. Swiftly Tybalt's sword shot beneath his uplifted arm and into Mercutio's side.

Mercutio clutched the wound. 'What, are you hurt?' gasped Romeo.

'Aye, aye, a scratch, a scratch,' winced Mercutio, and turned suddenly very pale. 'Go fetch a surgeon,' he breathed, grey with pain.

'Courage, man,' urged Romeo, 'the hurt cannot be much.'

'No, it is not so deep as a well, nor so wide as a churchdoor, but it is enough, it will serve … Ask for me tomorrow and you shall find me a grave man.' Mercutio gasped, and staggered a little, reaching for Benvolio's arm. 'I am done for this world,' he cried. 'A plague on both your houses! A dog, a rat, a mouse, a cat to scratch a man to death!' he

47

yelled at Tybalt. 'Why the devil did you come between us, Romeo? I was hurt under your arm.'

In stricken misery, Romeo stared at his friend. 'I thought all for the best,' he whispered.

The black hatred that was so swiftly stealing Mercutio's life now seemed to gather about Romeo and push him on, and with a cry of fury for Mercutio he leapt on Tybalt, fighting with a demon passion before he could think again; and before the onslaught, murderous Tybalt fell dead.

Romeo looked at his bloody sword. He looked at Benvolio's white-faced panic, urging him to fly before the prince should come, for it was death for anyone who broke Verona's peace.

'Oh, I am fortune's fool,' gasped Romeo. Wed to Juliet only an hour ago, and now the killer of his wife's cousin! Love and Juliet should be beckoning him, now only death or flight could wave him on!

Even as he fled the square, the Prince of Verona came with soldiers, and with Montague and Capulet. Bitterly these enemies demanded justice for their side.

'For blood of ours, shed blood of Montague,' raged Juliet's mother. 'I beg for justice, which you, prince, must give. Romeo killed Tybalt.

Romeo must not live!'

The prince looked at her in silent anger. *Mercutio* was no Capulet or Montague felled by their hatred! He was the prince's kinsman. He should have been beyond the reach of this vile feud. Would this poison *never* end? From now on he would be deaf to all the pleas these Capulets and Montagues used so easily to excuse the bitter fruits of enmity! As Romeo had been stung to this brawl by Mercutio's death, so would he reduce the sentence of death: but to a punishment no less complete.

Romeo was banished from Verona for ever more, on pain of instant death should he return.

Juliet knew nothing of the fight. She knew only that she loved, and that night would bring her husband to her bed.

'Come, gentle night,' she coaxed, 'come, loving, black-browed night. Give me my Romeo; and, when he shall die, take him and cut him out in little stars and he will make the face of heaven so fine that all the world will be in love with night … '

She turned eagerly to Nurse, who seemed to bring some news. But there was something wrong! No joyous ecstasy at imminent wedding nights from Nurse, but wringing hands, and wailing words! 'Tybalt dead and Romeo banished!'

Banished! Juliet struggled to understand the word. 'To speak that word is as if father, mother, Tybalt, Romeo, Juliet, were all dead. "Romeo is *banished!*"' she cried. The man she longed to see, to love, to hold, gone from Verona for ever more!

At Friar Lawrence's cell Romeo too heard the prince's sentence on him. And he knew that banishment meant death, for it was banishment from Juliet, from life itself!

The friar spoke calming words: banishment was only banishment from Verona! 'Be patient,' he urged. 'The world is broad and wide.'

'There is no world without Verona walls,' cried Romeo.

'This is dear mercy from the prince,' Friar Lawrence protested.

'It is torture,' wildly Romeo rejected it. 'Heaven is here, where Juliet lives, and every cat and dog and little mouse may live here in heaven and look on her, but Romeo may not!'

In vain the friar tried to calm his black despair, but Romeo would hear none of it. What could the friar know? He was not young, in love with Juliet, married a short hour, killer of Tybalt, and now *banished*. What could the friar know of such depths of hopelessness?

But now Nurse came hurrying in with messages from Juliet. She waited in desperate loneliness to see Romeo before he had to go. Nurse and Lawrence urged him to go to her; but he must leave for Mantua before the dawn. And then the friar would make his marriage to Juliet known, try to reconcile the families and obtain a pardon from the prince, so that Romeo could come back to bask in happiness!

His spirits much revived by this hopeful plan, and armed with the friar's promise that he would send word to Romeo in Mantua, of Juliet, in Verona, Romeo went to meet his love.

Capulet was worried by the grief that seemed to seize his daughter at Tybalt's death.

Knowing nothing of the secret marriage to Romeo, he could not guess the true cause of her unhappiness, and he thought it sprang from far too deep a well of sorrow. He was anxious for his daughter's health, and wished to have her misery gone. What better way than to occupy her mind with being wed! What better way than to have her married, and quickly, too, to Paris! Having so made up his mind, he picked the day and told it to his astounded wife. On Thursday next, in two short days, Juliet would marry Paris.

'Go to Juliet, before you go to bed,' he told Lady Capulet. 'Prepare her, wife, for this wedding day.'

But Juliet was already locked in her

wedding night with her new husband, longingly denying the birdsongs of the dawn that would take him away from her.

'I must be gone and live, or stay and die,' murmured Romeo, yet hoping she would entice him back for one last minute of happiness.

'That light is not daylight,' she whispered back. 'I know it, I. It is some meteor that the sun throws out to be your torchbearer and light you on your way to Mantua.'

'I have more care to stay than will to go! Come death, and welcome,' Romeo cried, and folded her inside his arms.

But already the sky was paling and with the anxious arrival of Nurse, come to hurry them along, he pulled away and began to climb down from the balcony into the orchard. Was it just one short day ago that he had first exchanged his love with Juliet? He seemed now to have known her all his life!

He saw her pale face looking down and heard her paler whisper. 'Do you think that we shall ever meet again? Oh god, I think I see you, now you are below, as one dead in the bottom of a tomb! You look so pale.'

'And trust me, love, so do you. Dry sorrow drinks our blood.'

And then he was gone, nothing but the echoes of the night still in her ears and on her lips and in her arms.

A call startled her. Lady Capulet was at

her door! Why was she up at this strange hour? So late not to be in bed: so early to be up already!

Lady Capulet had much to tell, despite the hour: she had a scheme to follow Romeo, the killer of Tybalt, to Mantua with poison. Soon, he too would die. And other tidings which she delivered with all the certainty of Juliet's pleasure: in two days time she would be wed to Paris!

Juliet heard it through a mask: she let no look or word escape to tell of her love for Tybalt's killer, nor that she was a wife before ever Paris could lay claim on her.

Half in terror at the trap she saw, half in terror at her parents' anger when they knew, she cried, 'I wonder at this haste! I pray you, tell my father that I will not marry yet.'

'Here comes your father; tell him so yourself and see how he will take it at your hands!' her mother told her angrily.

'What, still in tears?' her father demanded brusquely. He turned on his wife in irritation.

'Have you delivered to her our decree?'

'Aye, sir, but she will none. She gives you thanks. I wish the fool were married to her grave!'

'How!' bellowed Capulet. 'Is she not proud? Does she not count her blessings, unworthy that she is, that we have brought so worthy a gentleman to be her bridegroom?'

'Not proud you have,' protested Juliet, in tears, 'but thankful that you have ...'

'How now, how now! What is this?' her father yelled. '"Proud" and "I thank you" and "I thank you not". Thank me no thankings nor proud me no prouds, but prepare yourself for Thursday next to go with Paris to St Peter's Church or I will drag you on a hurdle!'

'Good father, I beg you,' wept Juliet, 'hear me with patience.'

'Disobedient wretch! I tell you what: get to church on Thursday or never after look me in the face: speak not, reply not, do not answer me; my fingers itch! God's bread,' raged Capulet. 'It makes me mad: day, night, hour, tide, time, work, play, alone, in company, all my care has been to have her married: and having now provided a suitable gentleman, to have her answer, "I'll not wed, I cannot love, I am too young, I pray you, pardon me!" I do not jest,' he hissed at her, 'if you will not wed, you may hang, beg, starve, die in the streets, for by my soul I'll never take you in!'

Juliet sat trembling in the silence behind his departing back.

'Oh, sweet mother, cast me not away,' she begged. 'Delay this marriage for a month, a week; or if you do not, make my bridal bed in that dim monument of death where Tybalt lies!'

'Talk not to me,' her mother waved her

off, 'for I'll not speak a word. Do as you will, for I have done with you.'

Juliet sank beneath a tide of hopelessness. All helping hands withdrawn! All roads to Romeo cut off and only one path open – marriage to another man!

She fled to Friar Lawrence's cell. The friar trembled at the dangers now looming before them all. A desperate plan took shape within his brain, fraught with a kind of horror. But Juliet was ready for anything to keep her faith as Romeo's wife.

Friar Lawrence gave her a potion: drink it, and she would seem to die, while all the while she only slept. This sleep with the look of death would last for forty-two hours; so, when they came to rouse her for the wedding, they would think her dead! According to long-established custom, they would lay her body in the tomb where the bodies of all the Capulets lay.

Meantime, the friar would send word to Romeo in Mantua. Romeo would hurry to the tomb to greet her when she woke, and carry her away with him to safety!

Awash with sudden hope, Juliet seized the friar's potion and hurried to her room.

The household was in a flurry such as there had never been before. One more day to prepare a wedding feast! Old Capulet gave orders for the festivities, while watching for some change of heart in Juliet.

And so there seemed to be! She came from Friar Lawrence all smiles, begging his pardon, and saying she would now be ruled by him!

'Send for Paris,' Capulet roared in triumph. 'I'll have this knot knit up tomorrow morning.'

'No, not till Thursday,' Lady Capulet begged her headstrong husband. 'We will be short in our supplies: it's nearly night!'

But he would have no contradiction. 'We'll go to church tomorrow.' His heart soared, so light it felt now that his wayward daughter had seen the error of her ways.

Juliet was alone. The silence filled her with a faint cold fear, like the creeping chill of tombs to which she would shortly give herself. It almost froze the heat of life in her. So suddenly to be faced with this! No time to think!

A thousand fears grimaced in her mind: what if the friar's potion did not work? She seized her dagger and held it up: why then, this would have to do the task!

What if she woke before she was

rescued, trapped in a tomb with only dead people to keep her company? Perhaps the loathsome foulness of the air would strangle her, or send her mad …

She pushed the visions back, and with a rush of courage raised the potion. 'Romeo, I come,' she whispered to the silence. 'This I drink to you.'

In Mantua, Romeo knew nothing of all this. He neither knew of Friar Lawrence's secret potion to make Juliet seem dead, nor that her father insisted that she marry Paris now.

His servant brought him only the news that Juliet was dead, found lifeless on the morning of her marriage.

The words broke upon him like the ice of his own death.

'Is it really so?' he breathed. 'Then I defy you, stars! I will go there tonight …'

'Sir, have patience,' his servant begged. 'Your looks are pale and wild.'

Romeo brushed his worries off, and urged him away to find horses for the journey to Verona.

'Well, Juliet, I will lie with you tonight,' he told her, in his head. A plan had taken hold of him, and now he had no other purpose in his life. Quickly he found a man in Mantua to sell him a deadly poison. 'Come, poison,' he spoke softly to the fatal bottle in his hand. 'Go with me to Juliet's grave, for there I must use you.'

Friar Lawrence hurried to the tomb where Juliet lay, armed with an iron bar to open it. His heart pounded with misery and fright. The messenger sent to tell Romeo that Juliet was not dead, only asleep, had not reached him! Both messenger and letter had been put in quarantine against the plague, and only just released.

So now the friar hastened to reach Juliet. She would wake soon, alone, trapped in the tomb. He must rescue her before she died of fright! Then, he would write again to Romeo and keep Juliet in his cell until Romeo could come to take her.

'Poor living corpse,' he wept, 'closed in a dead man's tomb!'

There was another visitor to the tomb that night. Paris knew nothing of Juliet's love for Romeo, nor of her terror at the marriage planned with him. He wept to lose her on their wedding day, and he came to lay flowers on the tomb and weep his private tears.

A third figure was entering the graveyard shadows. It was Romeo, fired by a grim light within which made his servant tremble.

'Whatever you hear or see, stand well away and do not interrupt me in my course,' Romeo gave orders to his servant. 'Do not return and pry, or by heaven I will tear you joint by joint and strew this hungry churchyard with your limbs!'

'I will be gone, sir, and not trouble you,' the servant hastily assured him. But he hid, to wait, for fear of what his desperate master planned.

Paris, sheltering behind the Capulet tomb, saw only that the Montague who had killed Juliet's cousin and made her take her life, now tried to open the tomb and desecrate it. With a shout of rage, he drew his sword and rushed to stop him.

And Romeo, knowing only that no one must stop him reaching Juliet's side, brought the intruder down.

'Oh, I am killed,' Paris gasped. 'If you be merciful, open the tomb and lay me with Juliet.'

Romeo saw now who he had killed, and understood that this man too loved Juliet. Sorrowfully, he lifted him and carried him into the tomb, and laid him gently on the floor.

Then he rose, and climbed on to the cold stone slab where Juliet lay, and knelt with her.

She lay so warmly beautiful. He did not see the crimson blush of her lips or fresh bloom of her cheeks as life, only as her beauty flaming for him even in her death. He could almost believe that Death itself loved her, and kept her in her glory here, to be his bride.

But Romeo would defy even Death, for he would stay with her and never leave this palace of dim night!

He lifted her then to his last embrace, sealed her lips with a kiss that would never end; and then he raised the poison to his lips and drank, and fell across her body, dead.

Friar Lawrence panted through the graveyard. He found Romeo's servant, and such a terror filled him as he had never known. He saw the bloodstains at the entrance to the tomb, the gory sword flung down, ran in and saw Romeo's lifeless corpse, and bloody Paris too.

Above this grim monument to death, Juliet began to stir. She saw the friendly face of Friar Lawrence, and smiled. 'Oh, comfortable friar, where is my lord? I do remember well where I should be, and here I am! But where is Romeo?'

Bereft of words, the friar shrank from the sight that greeted Juliet's waking eyes. He heard a noise outside, 'Lady, come from that nest of death,' he begged. 'Come, come away! Your husband lies there dead, and Paris too. Come, I'll put you in a sisterhood of holy nuns. Stay not to question,' he pleaded again. 'Good Juliet, I dare no longer stay.'

'Go,' said Juliet, 'for I will not away.'

A vast blackness filled her, as though the dark chill of death had already taken her. There was no world outside this place: no world beyond this tomb, where Romeo lay …

She found the cup of poison in his hand: no drop in it to help her on her way! She kissed his lips: no poison clung to them, only the warmth of life just gone.

But here his dagger waited, like a friend.

'Oh happy dagger!' she cried. 'This is your sheath!' and as the sounds of people running to the tomb broke in upon her world of timelessness, she stabbed herself and fell dead on Romeo, locked in her last embrace.

Capulet and Montague gathered around those they had buried with their hate. The sight of their children's deaths was like a bell that tolled their own deaths in this world of viciousness in which they revelled. And the sight of death was now the bell that tolled them back from it.

'Where be these enemies?' the Prince of Verona cried. 'Capulet! Montague! See what a scourge is laid upon your hate!' He looked at the body of Paris, so swiftly following Mercutio. 'And I too,' he mourned, 'for winking on your quarrels, have lost a brace of kinsmen. All are punished.'

But the tolling bell was heard by those who had till now heard nothing. Capulet reached a hand across to Montague. Each swore to raise a statue in pure gold in honour of the other's child; so would all know the tale of Romeo and Juliet, who fell before the venom of an ancient war, and only whose deaths had sounded the final call to peace.

Schools Library and Infomation Services

S00000689025